The Usborne
Little Book of
Christmas
Cooking

Rebecca Gilpin, Leonie Pratt
and Catherine Atkinson

Designed by Josephine Thompson,
Non Figg, Amanda Gulliver,
Katrina Fearn and Doriana Berkovic

Illustrated by Kim Lane, Sue Stitt,
Molly Sage and Non Figg

Photographs by Howard Allman

Americanization: Carrie Armstrong
American expert: Barbara Tricinella

Contents

Some of these cookies are decorated with sparkly writing icing, as well as white icing.

Snowflake cookies

To make about 12 cookies, you will need:

    6 tablespoons butter, softened
    ¼ cup powdered sugar
    1 cup all-purpose flour
    white writing icing
    a 2½ inch round cookie cutter

Before you start, grease two cookie sheets with cooking oil. You will need to heat your oven to 350°F in step 3.

❄ Keep the cookies in an airtight container and eat them within a week.

Flatten the dough a little before you wrap it.

1. Put the butter into a bowl and stir it until it is creamy. Sift the powdered sugar in and stir the mixture until it is smooth.

2. Sift the flour into the bowl and stir it in with a wooden spoon. Then, using your hands, squeeze the mixture to make a dough.

3. Wrap the dough in plastic foodwrap and put it in a refrigerator for 30 minutes. While the dough chills, turn on your oven.

Try drawing different
patterns on some
of the cookies.

4. Dust a rolling pin and a clean work surface with flour. Then, roll out the dough until it is about ¼ inch thick.

5. Cut out lots of circles with the cutter. Then, squeeze the scraps into a ball and roll it out. Cut out more circles.

6. When you have used all the dough, put the circles onto the cookie sheets. Then, bake the cookies for 10-12 minutes.

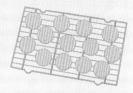

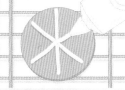

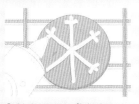

7. Leave the cookies on the cookie sheets for two minutes. Then, move them onto a wire rack with a spatula and let them cool.

8. Draw a line down the middle of one cookie with white writing icing. Draw two more lines crossing over the first one, like this.

9. Make a snowflake by adding small lines of writing icing across the ends of the lines. Then, decorate all the other cookies, too.

Pretty pear pies

To make 12 pies, you will need:

13-15oz package of ready-made pie crust
  taken out of the refrigerator 20 minutes
  before you start.
1 small orange
1½ teaspoons butter
2 tablespoons brown sugar
3 tablespoons dried cranberries
½ teaspoon ground cinnamon

2 soft, sweet pears or four
  canned pear halves
milk for glazing
powdered sugar for dusting
12-hole muffin tray
a 3 inch round cookie cutter
  and a star-shaped cutter

Before you start, grease two cookie sheets with cooking oil.
You will need to heat your oven to 375°F in step 5.

❄ Keep the pies in an airtight container and eat them within five days.

You don't need the other half
of the orange.

You don't need to peel
canned pears.

1. Grate half the rind from the orange using the fine holes on a grater. Cut the orange in half and squeeze the juice from one half.

2. Put the rind and one tablespoon of the orange juice into a pan. Then, add the butter, brown sugar, cranberries and cinnamon.

3. Carefully peel the pears with a vegetable peeler. Cut them into quarters and cut out the cores. Then, cut the quarters into small pieces.

Keep stirring the mixture so that it doesn't stick.

Dust the rolling pin with flour, too.

Cut the circles as close together as you can.

4. Put the pear pieces into the pan. Gently heat the mixture on low heat for 10 minutes. Take it off the heat and let it cool.

5. Turn on your oven. Dust a clean work surface with flour and roll out the pastry until it is about ¼ inch thick.

6. With the round cutter, cut 12 circles from the dough. Press the scraps together to make a ball and put it aside.

The milk will make the pastry shiny when it is cooked.

The pies can be eaten warm or cold.

7. Press the circles into the pans in the muffin tray. Then, put a heaped teaspoon of the pear mixture into each one.

8. Roll out the ball of dough and cut out 12 stars with the star cutter. Lay the stars on the pies, then brush milk over them.

Wear oven mitts.

9. Bake the pies for 20 minutes, until they are golden. Then, lift them out and leave them in the tray to cool for 10 minutes.

10. Using a blunt knife, lift the pies onto a plate. Put a little powdered sugar into a sieve and sprinkle the sugar over the pies.

You could serve the pies with a spoonful of whipped cream.

Christmas fairy crowns

To make 16 cookies,
you will need:

4 tablespoons butter
3 tablespoons corn syrup
1¼ cups self-rising flour
½ teaspoon ground cinnamon
½ teaspoon baking soda
1 tablespoon brown sugar
2 tablespoons milk
writing icing and candy for
  decorating

Before you start, grease two
cookie sheets with cooking oil.
You will need to heat your oven
to 350°F in step 5.

❄ Keep the cookies in an airtight
   container and eat them within
   three days.

1. Cut the butter into
cubes and put them into
a small pan. Add the corn
syrup, then gently heat
the pan on low heat.

2. Stir the mixture every
now and then, until it has
just melted. Then, take the
pan off the heat and let it
cool for three minutes.

*Flatten the dough a little
before you wrap it.*

3. Sift the flour, cinnamon
and baking soda into a
bowl and stir in the brown
sugar. Make a hollow in the
middle with a spoon.

4. Carefully pour the butter
and syrup mixture into the
hollow. Add the milk and
stir everything until you
have made a dough.

5. Wrap the dough in
plastic foodwrap and put
it in a refrigerator for 15
minutes. While it chills,
turn on your oven.

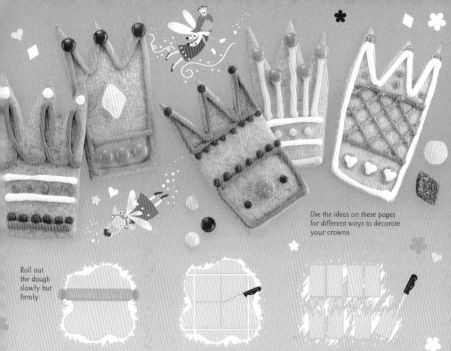

Use the ideas on these pages for different ways to decorate your crowns.

Roll out the dough slowly but firmly.

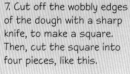

6. Dust a rolling pin and a clean work surface with some flour. Roll out the dough until it is slightly thinner than ¼ inch.

7. Cut off the wobbly edges of the dough with a sharp knife, to make a square. Then, cut the square into four pieces, like this.

8. Cut each piece in half, to make a rectangle. Then, make each rectangle into a crown by cutting out two small triangles at the top.

Use a spatula.

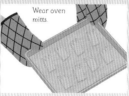

Wear oven mitts.

Stick on candy with dots of icing.

9. Squeeze the scraps into a ball and roll it out. Cut out more crowns, then put all of the crowns onto the cookie sheets.

10. Bake the crowns for 8-10 minutes. Carefully lift them out of the oven and leave them on the cookie sheets for five minutes.

11. Lift the crowns onto a wire rack with a spatula, and let them cool. Then, decorate them with writing icing and candy for jewels.

Shining star cookies

To make about 20 cookies, you will need:

½ cup brown sugar
⅓ cup soft margarine
a small egg
1¼ cups all-purpose flour
1 teaspoon allspice
different flavors of hard candy

a large star-shaped
  cookie cutter
a fat drinking straw
a small round cookie cutter,
  a little bigger than the candy
a large baking tray

Preheat your oven to 350°F.

❄ The cookies need to be kept in an airtight
  container and eaten within three days.

Thread thin ribbon
through the holes.

1. Put the sugar and margarine into a large bowl. Stir them together with a wooden spoon, until the mixture is smooth.

2. Break the egg into a separate bowl. Use a fork to stir the egg hard, until the yolk and the white are mixed together.

3. Mix half of the beaten egg into the mixture in the bowl, a little at a time. You don't need the other half of the egg mixture.

4. Sift the flour and allspice through a sieve into the bowl. Then, mix everything together really well, using a wooden spoon.

5. Use your hands to squeeze the mixture together to make a dough. Then, squeeze the dough into a large ball.

6. Dust a clean work surface and a rolling pin with flour. Then, roll out the ball of dough until it is about ¼ inch thick.

Don't eat the cookies if
you hang them on a
Christmas tree.

Use a
spatula.

7. Draw around a cookie sheet on wax paper. Cut out the shape and put it in the sheet. Cut stars from the dough and put them on the sheet.

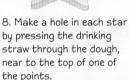

8. Make a hole in each star by pressing the drinking straw through the dough, near to the top of one of the points.

9. Use the small cookie cutter to cut a hole in the middle of each star. The hole should be slightly bigger than the candy.

10. Squeeze the scraps into a ball. Roll it out and cut more stars. Put them on the cookie sheet and make holes and circles in them.

11. Put a candy into the middle of each star. Put the cookie sheet on the middle shelf of the oven and bake the stars for 12 minutes.

12. Wearing oven mitts, take the cookies out of the oven. Leave them on the baking tray until they have cooled.

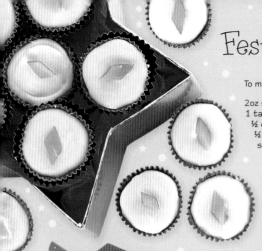

Festive fruit cups

To make 12 festive fruit cups, you will need:

2oz sweetened dried pineapple or mango
1 tablespoon pineapple or orange juice
½ cup semi-sweet or milk chocolate chips
½ cup white chocolate chips
small foil or double thickness paper candy cups

❄ Keep the fruit cups in an airtight container
and eat them within five days.

1. Put the pineapple or mango onto a cutting board. Then, using a sharp knife, carefully cut the fruit into tiny pieces.

2. Put about a quarter of the chopped fruit aside. Put the rest into a small bowl, and add the fruit juice. Stir it well.

3. Cover the bowl with plastic foodwrap. Then, leave the fruit for half an hour or until it has soaked up the juice.

Do this while the fruit is soaking.

4. Fill a large pan a quarter full of water. Heat the pan until the water bubbles, then remove the pan from the heat.

5. Put the semi-sweet or milk chocolate chips into a heatproof bowl. Wearing oven mitts, carefully put the bowl into the pan.

Wear oven mitts when you lift the bowl out.

6. Stir the chocolate with a metal spoon until it has melted. Lift the bowl out of the pan and leave it to cool for three minutes.

Spread the chocolate all the way up the sides.

7. Spread chocolate over the inside of the candy cups cases with a teaspoon. Put them in a refrigerator for 20 minutes, until firm.

8. Use a teapoon to put a little of the soaked fruit into each chocolate cup. Fill each cup until it is just over half full.

9. Follow steps 4-6 to melt the white chocolate chips in the same way as you melted the milk chocolate chips.

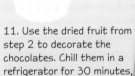

10. Spoon the melted white chocolate into the milk chocolate cups so that it completely covers the fruit.

11. Use the dried fruit from step 2 to decorate the chocolates. Chill them in a refrigerator for 30 minutes, then peel off the cups.

You could put the fruit cups in a pretty box and give them to someone as a gift.

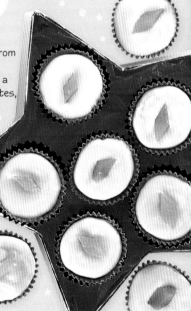

Little Christmas trees

You could arrange
the presents
around the trees.

To make 10 trees and 16 presents, you will need:

2 cups self-rising flour
1 cup soft margarine
4 tablespoons milk
1 level teaspoon baking powder
1 cup sugar
2-3 drops vanilla
4 medium eggs
a 9 x 13 inch baking pan

For the decorations:
⅔ cup butter, softened
2½ cups powdered sugar
1 teaspoon of vanilla
green, pink and yellow
  food coloring
small candy

Preheat your oven to 350°F.

❄ The cakes need to be stored in an airtight container and eaten within three days.

Wipe oil on
top of the
paper, too.

Use a
wooden
spoon to
stir the
mixture.

1. Draw around the baking
pan on wax paper and cut
out the shape. Wipe oil
inside the pan, then put the
paper into the pan.

2. Sift the flour through a
sieve into a large mixing
bowl. Add the margarine,
milk, baking powder, sugar
and vanilla.

3. Break the eggs into a
small bowl and mix them
with a fork. Add them to
the large bowl and stir the
mixture until it is smooth.

Make trunks for
the trees from
chocolate bars
or cookies.

Be careful – the cake will be hot.

Use a sieve.

4. Spoon the mixture into the pan and smooth the top. Bake it for 40-45 minutes, until the middle is springy when you press it.

5. After five minutes, lift the cake out of the pan and let it cool. For the icing, put the butter into a bowl and stir it until it is creamy.

6. Add the powdered sugar, a little at a time, stirring it in each time. Stir in the vanilla. Put three quarters of the icing in another bowl.

To make the color stronger, add more coloring, a drop at a time.

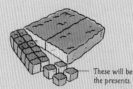
These will be the presents.

Press on candy to decorate.

7. Mix a few drops of green food coloring into the icing. Divide the rest of the icing in half. Add a different color to each half and mix it in.

8. Cut a strip 3 inches wide from one end of the cake. Cut it into 16 small squares. Then, cut the cake in half along its length.

9. Cut each strip into five triangles, for the trees. Ice them using the green icing. Then, ice the presents with the other colors of icing.

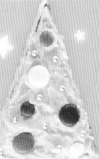

Mini florentines

To make about 18 mini florentines, you will need:

18 maraschino or candied cherries
18 unsalted mixed whole nuts, such as halved walnuts or pecans*
½ cup semi-sweet or milk chocolate chips
½ cup white chocolate chips
a cookie sheet lined with wax paper

✧ Keep the florentines in an airtight container, in a
  refrigerator, and eat them within four days.

* Don't give these to anyone
who is allergic to nuts.

1. Put the cherries in a
sieve. Rinse them under
warm running water to
remove the syrup. Pat them
dry with a paper towel.

2. Put the cherries onto a
cutting board. Carefully cut
the cherries into small
pieces, using a sharp knife.
Then, chop the nuts too.

3. Fill a large pan a quarter
full of water. Heat the pan
gently until the water
bubbles, then remove it
from the heat.

4. Put the semi-sweet or milk chocolate chips into a heatproof bowl. Wearing oven mitts, carefully put the bowl into the pan.

5. Stir the chocolate with a metal spoon until it has melted. Wearing oven mitts, carefully lift the bowl out of the pan.

6. Spoon a teaspoon of melted chocolate onto the wax paper. Make it into a neat circle, using the back of the spoon.

7. Gently press pieces of cherry and nut into the chocolate. Make more circles of chocolate and decorate them.

8. Follow steps 3-5 to melt the white chocolate chips. Make more circles with the white chocolate. Then, decorate them, too.

9. Put the florentines in a refrigerator for half an hour. Then, when the chocolates have hardened, carefully peel them off the paper.

Christmas mice

To make about eight large mice, five medium mice and three baby mice, you will need:

2 cups powdered sugar
1 cup condensed milk
3 cups shredded coconut
red food coloring
candy for ears
silver cake-decorating balls
red licorice strings

❄ Keep the mice in an airtight container and eat them within ten days.

More coloring will make the mixture a stronger pink.

1. Sift the powdered sugar through a sieve into a large bowl. Add the condensed milk and the coconut, then stir everything together.

2. Put the mixture into two bowls. Mix a few drops of red food coloring into each bowl. Then, add a little more coloring to one of the bowls.

For baby mice, use a teaspoon for the body

3. Dip a clean tablespoon into some warm water and let it drip a little. Then, lift a spoonful of the mixture from one of the bowls.

4. Pat the top of the spoonful to make it smooth. Then, turn it over onto a piece of plastic foodwrap and lift off the spoon.

You can use tiny candy if you don't have any silver balls.

5. Pinch a nose at the thinner end of the spoon shape. Then, add candy for the mouse's ears and silver balls for eyes.

6. Push a piece of licorice under the shape, for a tail. Make lots more mice from the mixture and leave them to harden on a plate.

Use a dessertspoon for a medium mouse.

Snowball truffles

To make about 15 truffles, you will need:

1 cup white chocolate chips
2 tablespoons unsalted butter
15 vanilla wafers
4 tablespoons shredded coconut
small paper candy cups

❄ Keep the truffles in a refrigerator, in an airtight
   container, and eat them within five days.

1. Fill a large pan a
quarter full of water and
heat it until the water
bubbles. Then, remove
the pan from the heat.

2. Put the chocolate chips
and the butter into a
heatproof bowl. Wearing
oven mitts, carefully put
the bowl into the pan.

Keep stirring until
everything has
melted.

3. After two minutes, stir
the chocolate and butter
until they melt. Wearing
oven mitts, carefully lift
the bowl out of the water.

4. Crumble the wafers into
fine crumbs. Add the
crumbs to the chocolate
mixture and stir everything
well with a wooden spoon.

You could put the truffles in a gift box and give them to someone for Christmas.

5. Spread the coconut onto a plate. Scoop up some of the chocolate mixture with a teaspoon and put it into the coconut.

6. Using your fingers, roll the chocolate mixture in the coconut to make a ball. When it is covered, put it into a paper cup.

7. Make more truffles with the rest of the mixture. Then, put them onto a plate and put them in a refrigerator for one hour.

Chocolate fudge

To make about 36 squares, you will need:

½ cup full-fat cream cheese
2 cups powdered sugar
1 level tablespoon cocoa powder
½ cup semi-sweet chocolate chips
2 tablespoons butter
a shallow 8 inch square cake pan

❋ Keep the fudge in an airtight container
in a refrigerator, and eat it within a week.

Use a pencil to draw around the pan.

1. Lay the cake pan on a sheet of wax paper and draw around it. Then, cut out the square, just inside the line.

2. Use a paper towel to wipe cooking oil onto the sides and bottom of the pan. Press in the paper and wipe the top with oil.

3. Put the cream cheese into a bowl. Sift the powdered sugar and cocoa through a sieve into the bowl. Mix everything together well.

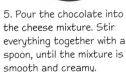

4. Melt the chocolate and butter as in steps 1-3 on page 20. Then, stir in a tablespoon of the cream cheese mixture.

5. Pour the chocolate into the cheese mixture. Stir everything together with a spoon, until the mixture is smooth and creamy.

6. Carefully spoon the fudge into the pan, and push it into the corners. You may need to use your fingers to do this.

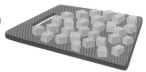

7. Smooth the top of the fudge with the back of a spoon. Put the pan in the refrigerator for two hours, or until the fudge is firm.

8. Loosen the edges of the fudge with with a blunt knife. Then, turn it out onto a cutting board and remove the wax paper.

9. Cut the fudge into 36 squares. Put the fudge in an airtight container and chill it in a refrigerator for two more hours.

Snow-covered crispies

To make about 20 crispies, you will need:

1½ sticks butter, softened
¼ cup brown sugar
1 egg
1 teaspoon of vanilla
1¼ cups self-rising flour
corn flakes
⅔ cup white chocolate chips
sugar sprinkles

Before you start, grease two
cookie sheets with cooking oil.
Cut a large piece of baking
parchment and put it on a
cutting board.
Preheat your oven to 375°F.

❄ These crispies are best eaten on the day you make them.

Stir the mixture hard.

1. Put the butter into a
large bowl and stir it until
it is creamy. Add the sugar
and stir the mixture until
it is fluffy.

2. Break the egg into a
cup and add the vanilla.
Stir the mixture with a
fork, then pour half of it
into the bowl.

3. Stir in the egg mixture.
Then, add the rest and
stir that in, too. Sift the
flour into the bowl, then
stir everything well.

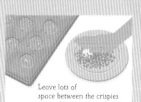

*Leave lots of
space between the crispies.*

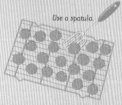

Use a spatula.

4. Crush some corn flakes
a little with your fingers
and put them onto a plate.
Scoop up a teaspoon of the
mixture and put it on top.

5. Roll the mixture in the
corn flakes to cover it. Put
it on a greased cookie
sheet, then make more
crispies in the same way.

6. Bake the crispies for
12-14 minutes. Leave
them on the trays for two
minutes, then lift them
onto a wire rack to cool.

7. Fill a large pan a quarter full of water and heat it until the water bubbles. Then, remove the pan from the heat.

8. Put the chocolate chips into a heatproof bowl. Then, wearing oven mitts, carefully put the bowl into the pan of water.

Wear oven mitts.

9. After two minutes, stir the chocolate chips with a metal spoon until they have melted. Carefully lift the bowl out of the water.

10. Put the crispies onto the cutting board. Then, spread a teaspoon of the melted chocolate over each crispy.

11. Sprinkle sugar sprinkles over the crispies. Put them in the refrigerator for 20 minutes, until the chocolate has set.

25

Christmas fairy castle cake

For a cake that will serve 8-10 people, you will need:

1½ sticks margarine, softened
1⅓ cups sugar
3 tablespoons milk
1 teaspoon vanilla
1¾ cups self-rising flour
3 medium eggs
a shallow 7 x 11 inch cake pan

For the decorations:
2 cups powdered sugar
2 tablespoons milk
1 drop of red food coloring
writing icing
small candy

Preheat your oven to 350°F.

❄ Keep the cake in an airtight container or cover it in plastic foodwrap, and eat it within three days.

1. Lay the cake pan on a sheet of wax paper and draw around it with a pencil. Then, cut out the shape, just inside the line.

2. Use a paper towel to wipe some cooking oil on the bottom and sides of the pan. Press in the paper and wipe the top with oil.

3. Put the margarine and sugar into a large bowl. Mix the milk and vanilla together and pour them in. Then, sift the flour in, too.

Use a wooden spoon.

4. Break the eggs into a cup and mix them with a fork. Add them to the bowl and stir the mixture until it is smooth and creamy.

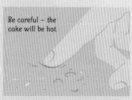

Be careful – the cake will be hot.

5. Spoon the mixture into the pan and smooth the top. Bake it for 30-35 minutes, until the middle is springy when you press it.

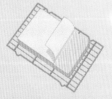

6. After five minutes, run a blunt knife around the cake. Turn it onto a wire rack and peel off the paper, then leave the cake to cool.

26

Put the strips on the board like this, to make three towers.

7. Put the cake on a board. Cut it into three strips and cut one strip in half. Move a long strip and the short strips onto another board.

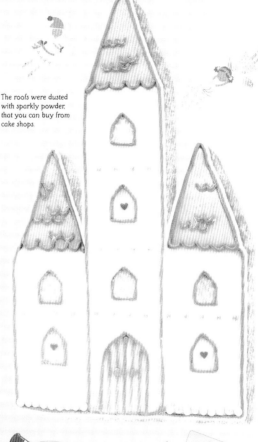

The roofs were dusted with sparkly powder, that you can buy from cake shops.

8. Cut the last strip into three equal pieces. Then, cut the pieces into tall triangles, for roofs. Put them on top of the towers.

The icing should be smooth.

9. Sift half the powdered sugar into a bowl. Stir in one tablespoon of milk, a little at a time, and spread the icing on the towers.

10. Mix the rest of the powdered sugar with a drop of red food coloring and one tablespoon of milk. Spread it over the roofs.

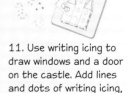

11. Use writing icing to draw windows and a door on the castle. Add lines and dots of writing icing, then press on candy.

Tiny Christmas cookies

To make about 65 tiny cookies, you will need:

4 tablespoons butter, softened
¼ cup powdered sugar
8 drops red food coloring
1½ teaspoon milk
¼ teaspoon vanilla
¾ cup all-purpose flour
little star and heart cookie cutters

Before you start, grease two cookie sheets with cooking oil.
Preheat your oven to 350°F.

✸ Keep the cookies in an airtight container and eat them within a week.

1. Put the butter into a bowl and stir it until it is creamy. Then, sift in the powdered sugar and stir everything well.

2. Add the food coloring to the mixture and stir it in well, until the mixture is pink. Then, add the milk and the vanilla.

Cut the shapes close together.

3. Sift the flour through a sieve into the bowl and stir everything together. Then, use your hands to squeeze the mixture into a dough.

4. Dust a rolling pin and a clean work surface with a little flour. Then, roll out the dough until it is about ¼ inch thick.

5. Use the cookie cutters to cut lots of shapes from the dough. Then, use a spatula to lift the shapes onto the cookie sheets.

6. Squeeze the scraps of dough together to make a ball. Roll out the dough again and cut more shapes. Put them onto the sheets.

7. Make patterns on some of the cookies by pushing the end of a toothpick into them. Don't worry if it goes all the way through.

Wear oven mitts.

8. Bake the cookies for six to eight minutes. Then, take them out of the oven and leave them on the sheets until they are cool.

Some of these cookies were dusted with powdered sugar when they were cool.

You could put some cookies into a gift box to give as a present.

Shortbread

To make eight pieces, you will need:

1½ cups all-purpose flour
½ cup butter, refrigerated, cut into chunks
½ cup sugar
8 inch shallow round pan

Preheat the oven to 300°F.

❄ Keep the shortbread in an airtight container
and eat it within three days.

1. Rub some butter onto a paper towel, then use it to grease the bottom and sides of the pan. Make sure it is all greased.

2. Sift the flour through a sieve into a large mixing bowl. Then, add the chunks of refrigerated butter to the bowl, too.

3. Mix in the butter so that it is coated in flour. Then, use your fingers to rub the butter into the flour, until it is like fine breadcrumbs.

Press the mixture against the side of the bowl.

4. Stir in the sugar with a wooden spoon. Hold the bowl with one hand and use your other hand to squeeze the mixture into a ball.

5. Press the mixture into the pan with your fingers. Then, use the back of a spoon to smooth the top and make it level.

6. Use a fork to press patterns and make holes around the edge. Then, cut the shortbread into eight pieces, using a blunt knife.

7. Bake the shortbread for 30 minutes, until it is golden. Leave it in the pan for 10 minutes, then put it onto a wire rack to cool.

Jeweled cupcakes

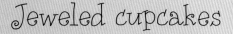

To make 12 cupcakes, you will need:

½ cup milk
¼ cup chocolate chips
¾ cup sugar
5 tablespoons butter, softened
1 medium egg
1¼ cups self-rising flour
paper muffin cups
12-hole muffin tray

For decorating:
6 tablespoons butter, softened
1½ cups powdered sugar, sifted
a few drops vanilla
2 teaspoons milk
small candy and sugar sprinkles

Before you start, put 12 paper cups into the pans in the muffin tray and preheat your oven to 375°F.

❄ Keep the cupcakes in an airtight container and eat them within two days.

Keep stirring so that the mixture does not stick.

1. Put the milk, chocolate chips and half of the sugar into a small pan. Then, gently heat the pan on low heat.

2. When the chocolate has melted, and the sugar has dissolved, take the pan off the heat. Then, leave the mixture to cool.

3. Put the butter into a large bowl and stir until it is creamy. Add the rest of the sugar and stir the mixture until it is fluffy.

4. Break the egg into a mug and stir it with a fork. Add half of the egg to the bowl and stir it in, then add the rest and stir that in, too.

5. Sift half of the flour through a sieve into the bowl. Pour in half of the chocolate mixture and stir it in with a wooden spoon.

Put the same amount of mixture into each cup.

Wear oven mitts.

Stir the mixture hard.

6. Sift in the remaining flour and add the rest of the chocolate mixture. Mix everything well and spoon the mixture into the cups.

7. Bake the cupcakes for 18 minutes, then take them out of the oven. After two minutes, put them onto a wire rack to cool.

8. For the icing, put the butter into a large bowl and stir it until it is creamy. Add some of the powdered sugar and stir it in.

9. Add the rest of the sugar, a little at a time, stirring it in well. Then, add the vanilla and milk, and stir them in.

10. Peel the paper cups off the cupcakes. Use a blunt knife to spread icing on top of them, then press on candy and spinkles.

Snow cloud meringues

To make about 30 meringues,
you will need:

2 eggs, at room temperature
½ cup granulated sugar
sugar sprinkles

Preheat your oven to 225°F.

❄️ Keep the meringues in an airtight
container and eat them within a week.

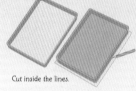

Cut inside the lines.

1. Draw around a cookie
sheet on baking parchment.
Cut out the shape and put
it in the sheet. Then, do the
same with another sheet.

2. Carefully break one egg
on the edge of a large
bowl. Then, pour it carefully
onto a saucer, so that the
egg yolk doesn't break.

You could use a yolk to make painted
cookies (see pages 44-45).

3. Hold a cup over the yolk
and carefully tip the
saucer over the bowl so
that the egg white
dribbles into it.

4. Repeat steps 2-3 with
the other egg so that
both egg whites are in the
bowl. You don't need the
egg yolks.

5. Whisk the egg whites
with a whisk until they are
really thick. They should
form stiff points when you
lift the whisk up.

6. Add a tablespoon of sugar to the egg whites and whisk it in well. Whisk in the rest of the sugar a tablespoon at a time.

7. Scoop up a teaspoon of the meringue mixture. Then, use another teaspoon to push it off onto one of the cookie sheets.

8. Make more meringues until you have used all the mixture. Then, sprinkle a few sugar sprinkles over each one.

9. Put the meringues into the oven and bake them for 40 minutes. Then, turn off the oven, leaving the meringues inside.

Wear oven mitts.

10. After 15 minutes, carefully lift the cookie sheets out of the oven. Leave the meringues on the sheets to cool.

35

Peppermint creams

To make about 25 peppermint creams, you will need:

2 cups powdered sugar
3 teaspoons of dried or pasteurized liquid egg
  white (mixed as directed on the package)
¼ teaspoon of peppermint flavoring
2 teaspoons lemon juice
red and green food coloring
small cookie cutters
a cookie sheet covered
  in plastic foodwrap

☼ Keep the peppermint creams in an airtight
  container and eat them within two weeks.

1. Sift the powdered sugar through a sieve into a large bowl. Then, make a small hollow in the middle of the sugar using a spoon.

2. Mix together the egg white, peppermint flavoring and lemon juice in a small bowl. Pour the mixture into the middle of the sugar.

3. Stir everything together using a blunt knife. Squeeze the mixture between your fingers until it is smooth, then cut it into two halves.

Add powdered sugar if
the mixture is sticky.

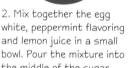

Use a sieve.

4. Put each half into a separate bowl. Add a few drops of red food coloring to one bowl, and a few drops of green to the other.

5. Use your fingers to mix in the red coloring. Wash your hands, then mix the green coloring into the mixture in the other bowl.

6. Sprinkle a little powdered sugar onto a clean work surface. Sprinkle some onto a rolling pin too, to stop the mixture from sticking.

You could put the
peppermints in boxes
to give as presents

Cut the shapes
close together

7. Roll out the pink mixture until it is about as thick as your little finger. Then, use small cookie cutters to cut out lots of shapes.

8. Lift the shapes onto the cookie sheet. Squeeze the scraps into a ball and roll it out. Cut out more shapes and put them on the sheet.

9. Roll out the green mixture and cut out more shapes. Then, leave all the shapes on the sheet for an hour, to harden.

Starry jam tart

To make one jam tart, you will need:

12oz ready-made pie crust taken out of the
  refrigerator 10 minutes before you start.
about 2 tablespoons all-purpose flour
6 rounded tablespoons seedless raspberry
  or strawberry preserves
milk for glazing

8in shallow pie tin
a small star-shaped cookie cutter

Preheat your oven to 400°F.

❄ Keep the tart in an airtight container and eat it within three days.

You can use any
shape of cutter you
like. Stars and holly
leaves look very
Christmassy.

1. Sprinkle some all-purpose flour over a clean work surface and onto a rolling pin. This will stop the pastry from sticking.

2. Cut off a quarter of the dough. Then, wrap it in some plastic foodwrap and put it to the side until step 6.

Sift a little powdered sugar onto a slice of tart and serve it with whipped cream.

The rolling pin cuts off the extra dough.

3. Roll out the bigger piece of dough. Then, turn it around a little and roll it again to make a circle about 12 inches across.

4. Put the rolling pin at one side of the dough. Roll the dough around it and lift it up. Place the dough over the tin and unroll it.

5. Dip a finger into some flour and press the dough into the edges of the tin. Then, roll the rolling pin across the top.

6. Spoon the preserves into the dough crust. Spread it out with the back of a spoon. Roll out the other quarter of the dough.

Use a pastry brush.

7. Using the cutter, cut out about 12 shapes from the dough. Brush them with a little milk and place them on top of the preserves.

The pastry will be golden brown.

8. Bake the jam tart for 20 minutes. Wearing oven mitts, take the tart out of the oven. Let the preserves cool before serving.

Christmas tree cupcakes

To make 15 cupcakes, you will need:

2 cups all purpose flour
½ teaspoon salt
3 teaspoons baking powder
2 medium eggs
½ cup soft margarine
1¼ cups sugar
1 teaspoon vanilla
1 cup milk

For decorating:
¼ cup butter, softened
2 cups powdered sugar
2 teaspoons lemon juice or
  1 teaspoon vanilla
2 tablespoons milk
small candy and silver
  cake-decorating balls.
paper baking cups
two 12-hole muffin trays

Preheat your oven to 375°F.

❄ Keep the cupcakes in an airtight container and
  eat them within two days.

1. Sift the flour, salt and baking powder through a sieve into a large bowl. Break the eggs into a cup and stir them with a fork.

Stir until the mixture is smooth and creamy.

2. Add the eggs to the bowl. Then, add the magarine, sugar, vanilla and milk, and stir everything together using a wooden spoon.

3. Put 15 paper cups into the pans in the muffin trays. Then, use a spoon to half-fill each cup with the cake mixture.

Leave the cakes to cool.

4. Bake the cakes for 20 minutes. Wear oven mitts to take the cakes out of the oven. After five minutes move them onto a wire rack.

5. For the icing, put the butter into a large mixing bowl and stir it well using a fork. Continue until it is really creamy.

6. Add some of the powdered sugar and stir it in. Then, add the rest of the sugar, a little at a time, stirring it in each time.

7. Add the lemon juice or the vanilla to the bowl. Then, add the milk and stir everything together until the mixture is smooth.

Arrange the cupcakes into a tree shape, like this.

8. Use a blunt knife to spread some icing on top of each cake. Then, press on lots of candy to decorate the cakes.

You could make different patterns of candy on top of each cupcake.

Use a flaky chocolate bar as a tree trunk.

Iced gingerbread hearts

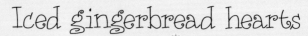

To make about 20 cookies, you will need:

2 cups all-purpose flour
2 teaspoons ground ginger
2 teaspoons baking soda
½ cup butter or margarine, cut into chunks
¾ cup brown sugar
1 medium egg
4 tablespoons maple syrup
white writing icing
silver cake-decorating balls
or small candy
a large heart-shaped cookie cutter

Before you start, grease two cookie sheets with
cooking oil and preheat your
oven to 375°F.

❄ Keep the cookies in an airtight container
and eat them within three days.

You could wrap some
cookies in tissue paper
or cellophane twists, to
give as a present.

1. Sift the flour, ground ginger and baking soda through a sieve into a large bowl. Add the butter or margarine chunks.

2. Use your fingers to rub the butter or margarine into the flour until it is like fine breadcrumbs. Then, stir in the sugar.

3. Break the egg into a small bowl and add the syrup. Using a fork, stir the mixture well, then add it to the large bowl.

4. Mix everything with a metal spoon to make a dough. Sprinkle flour onto a clean work surface, then put the dough onto it.

Do this until the dough is smooth.

5. Dust flour onto your hands, then stretch the dough by pushing it away from you. Fold the dough in half and repeat.

Sprinkle more flour onto the work surface.

6. Cut the dough in half and sprinkle flour onto a rolling pin. Roll out half the dough until it is about ¼ inch thick.

7. Use the heart-shaped cutter to cut out lots of hearts. Then, use a spatula to lift the hearts onto the cookie sheets.

8. Roll out the rest of the dough. Cut out more hearts and put them on the cookie sheets. Wearing oven mitts, put the trays in the oven.

9. Bake the cookies for 12-15 minutes, until they are golden brown. Wearing oven mitts, carefully lift the sheets from the oven.

10. Leave the cookies on the sheets for about 5 minutes. Then, use a spatula to lift them onto a wire rack and leave them to cool.

11. When the cookies are cold, draw lines across them with writing icing. Cross some of the lines over each other, like this.

12. Leave the icing for a few minutes, to harden. Then, press cake-decorating balls, or small candy into the icing, where the lines cross.

Painted cookies

To make about 15 cookies, you will need:

½ cup powdered sugar
½ cup soft margarine
the yolk from a large egg
¼ teaspoon vanilla
1¼ cups all-purpose flour
big cookie cutters

To decorate the cookies:
an egg yolk
different food colorings

Before you start, grease a cookie sheet
with cooking oil and preheat
the oven to 350°F.

❄ Keep the cookies in an airtight container
and eat within five days.

Use a
wooden
spoon.

1. Sift the powdered sugar through a sieve into a large bowl. Then, add the margarine and stir the mixture until it is smooth.

2. Add the large egg yolk and stir it in well. Then, add a few drops of vanilla. Stir the vanilla into the mixture well.

Flatten the dough a
little before you
wrap it.

3. Sift the flour into the mixture and stir it in with a wooden spoon. Then, use your hands to squeeze the mixture to make a dough.

4. Wrap the dough in plastic foodwrap. Then, put the dough in a freezer while you make the 'paint' to decorate the cookies.

Use the ideas on these pages to paint patterns on your cookies.

You could use festive cutters, such as holly shapes and bell shapes.

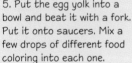

5. Put the egg yolk into a bowl and beat it with a fork. Put it onto saucers. Mix a few drops of different food coloring into each one.

6. Sprinkle flour over a clean work surface and onto a rolling pin. Then, roll out the dough until it is as thin as your little finger.

Use a clean paintbrush to paint the patterns.

7. Press out shapes using the cookie cutters. Use a spatula to lift them onto the cookie sheet. Squeeze the scraps into a ball.

8. Roll out the ball and cut out more shapes. Paint patterns on the cookies Then, bake the cookies in the oven for 10-12 minutes.

9. Wearing oven mitts, take the cookies out of the oven. Leave them for five minutes, then lift them onto a wire rack to cool.

Sparkly stars

To make 20 cookies, you will need:

3 tablespoons granulated sugar
2 drops red food coloring
6 tablespoons butter, softened
1 small lemon
2 tablespoons brown sugar
3 tablespoons honey
1 medium egg
1¼ cups all-purpose flour
medium and small star cutters

Before you start, grease two cookie sheets with cooking oil. You will need to heat your oven to 350°F in step 7.

❄ The cookies need to be stored in an airtight container and eaten within five days.

1. Put the sugar into a bowl, then add the food coloring. Stir the sugar until it is pink. Then, spread it on a plate to dry.

Use the fine holes on the grater

2. Put the butter into a large bowl and stir it until it is creamy. Then, grate the rind off the lemon and add the rind to the bowl.

3. Add the brown sugar and the honey to the bowl. Then, stir everything together well until the mixture is smooth.

4. Carefully break the egg on the edge of a bowl. Then, pour the egg carefully onto a saucer, so that the egg yolk doesn't break.

Keep the egg white for later

5. Put a cup over the yolk. Tip the saucer so that the egg white dribbles into a bowl. Then, stir the yolk into the honey mixture.

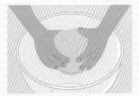

The flour will stop the dough from sticking.

6. Use a sieve to sift the flour into the mixture. Stir it in, then squeeze the mixture to make a dough. Wrap it in plastic foodwrap.

7. Chill the dough in a refrigerator for 30 minutes. Heat your oven while it chills. Dust a clean work surface and a rolling pin with flour.

Cut the stars close together

8. Roll out the dough until it is about ¼ inch thick. Then, use the medium cookie cutter to cut out lots of star shapes.

9. Use the small cutter to cut a star from the middle of each cookie. Press the scraps into a ball, roll it out and cut out more stars.

Wear oven mitts.

10. Brush a little egg white over each star and sprinkle pink sugar on top. Then, use a spatula to lift the stars onto the cookie sheets.

11. Bake the cookies for 8-10 minutes, then take them out of the oven. After five minutes, lift them onto a wire rack to cool.

Chocolate swirls

To make about 25 chocolate swirls, you will need:

2¼ cups powdered sugar
3 teaspoons of dried or pasteurized liquid
  egg white (mixed as directed on the packet)
1 teaspoon lemon juice
¼ teaspoon mint extract
1 tablespoon cocoa powder
2 teaspoons boiling water
½ teaspoon vanilla
a cookie sheet covered in plastic foodwrap

✿ The swirls need to be kept in an airtight container,
  in a refrigerator, and eaten within ten days.

Use a sieve.

1. Sift about one cup of
the powdered sugar into a
large bowl. Then, make a
small hollow in the middle
of the sugar with a spoon.

2. Mix half of the egg white
with the lemon juice and
peppermint in a small bowl.
Pour the mixture into the
hollow in the sugar.

3. Stir the mixture with a
blunt knife, then squeeze it
with your fingers until it is
smooth. Wrap the mixture
in plastic foodwrap.

If the mixture is a little dry, add a drop of water.

4. Sift the cocoa powder through a sieve into a large bowl. Add the water and vanilla, then, mix everything together well.

5. Add the rest of the egg white and stir it in. Sift the rest of the powdered sugar into the bowl. Then, stir the mixture with a blunt knife.

6. Squeeze the mixture until it is smooth. Wrap it in foodwrap, too. Then, put the two mixtures in a refrigerator for 10 minutes.

7. Sprinkle a little powdered sugar onto a clean work surface and a rolling pin. The powdered sugar stops the mixture from sticking.

8. Roll out the white mixture into a rectangle 8 inches by 6 inches. Then, do the same with the chocolate mixture.

9. Put the chocolate rectangle on top of the white one. Then, trim the edges with a knife to make them straight.

Roll the rectangle from one of the long edges.

10. Tightly roll the rectangle into a sausage. Then, wrap it in foodwrap and put it in a refrigerator for about 10 minutes.

11. Take off the foodwrap. Then, use a sharp knife to carefully cut the sausage into slices about as thick as your little finger.

12. Put the swirls onto the foodwrap-covered cookie sheet. Then, leave the swirls in a cool, dry place to harden overnight.

49

Coconut cookies

To make about 20 cookies, you will need:

1 stick butter, softened
1 teaspoon vanilla
½ cup powdered sugar
1 cup all-purpose flour
3 tablespoons cornmeal
¼ cup shredded coconut
about 2 tablespoons of seedless raspberry or
  strawberry preserves

Before you start, grease two cookie sheets with cooking oil.
Preheat your oven to 350°F.

✦ Keep the cookies in an airtight container
  and eat them within a week.

1. Put the butter into a large mixing bowl and stir it with a wooden spoon until it is creamy. Then, stir in the vanilla.

2. Sift the powdered sugar through a sieve into the bowl. Then, stir the mixture well until it is smooth and creamy.

3. Sift the flour and the cornmeal into the bowl. Then, add the coconut and stir everything well to make a soft dough.

4. Rub some flour on your hands. Then, scoop up a little of the dough with a teaspoon and roll it into a smooth ball.

5. Make more balls and put them on the greased cookie sheets. Leave spaces between the balls, because they spread as they cook.

6. Push your little finger into the middle of each ball, to make a hollow. Push it in up to the first knuckle, like this.

Wear oven mitts

7. Bake the cookies for 12-14 minutes. Carefully lift them out of the oven, then leave them to cool on the cookie sheets.

8. When the cookies have cooled, sift some powdered sugar over them. Then, use a teaspoon to fill the holes with preserves.

Crinkly Christmas pies

To make 12 pies, you will need:

4 apples
3 tablespoons orange juice
½ cup dried cranberries or raisins
2 teaspoons sugar
½ teaspoon ground cinnamon
4oz fillo dough (about 6 sheets)
2 tablespoons butter
powdered sugar for dusting
a baking tray with shallow pans or 12-hole muffin tray

Preheat the oven to 375°F.

❄ Keep the pies in an airtight container and eat them within five days.

You may need to ask someone to help you.

Put the lid back on after you've stirred the apples.

Stir the mixture often.

1. Carefully peel the apples with a vegetable peeler. Cut them into quarters and cut out the cores. Then, cut the quarters into small pieces.

2. Put the pieces into a pan and add the juice. Cover the pan with a lid. Heat the pan on a very low heat for 20 minutes, stirring often.

3. Stir in the dried fruit, sugar and cinnamon. Cook the mixture for about five minutes, then take it off the heat.

Use a pastry brush.

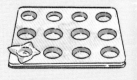

4. Unwrap the dough. Then, keeping the sheets together, cut them into six pieces, like this. Cover them with foodwrap.

5. Put the butter into a small pan and melt it on low heat. Brush a little butter over one of the dough squares.

6. Gently press the square into a hole in the tray, so that the buttered side faces up. Then, brush butter onto another square.

Eat the pies warm or cold.

Overlap the dough sheets so that they look like a star.

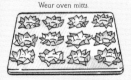

7. Put the second square on top of the first one, so the corners overlap a little. Add a third square, too. Fill all the holes in this way.

Wear oven mitts.

Heat the mixture until it bubbles slightly.

Use a small sieve if you have one.

8. Bake the cases on the middle shelf of the oven for 10 minutes. Take them out, then leave them to cool for five minutes.

9. Take the cases out of the tray and put them onto a large plate. Heat the apple mixture again for about two minutes.

10. Spoon the apple mixture into the cases, so that they are almost full. Sift a little powdered sugar over the pies.

Frosty fudge

To make about 50 pieces of fudge, you will need:

2⅔ cups powdered sugar
6 tablespoons unsalted butter
4 teaspoons milk
½ teaspoon vanilla
2 cups pink and white marshmallows (you can use jumbo or miniature ones for this recipe)
2 tablespoons sugar sprinkles
a shallow 7 inch square pan or loaf tin

❄ Keep the fudge in a refrigerator, in an airtight container, and eat it within a week.

You can use non-stick cooking spray

Put the bowl to the side until step 6.

1. Lay the pan on a piece of wax paper. Draw around it with a pencil, then cut out the square, just inside the line.

2. Use a paper towel to wipe cooking oil onto the sides and bottom of the pan. Press in the paper square and wipe it with oil.

3. Sift the powdered sugar through a sieve into a large bowl. Then, make a small hollow in the middle of the sugar with a spoon.

Don't cut miniature marshmallows in half

4. Put the butter, milk and vanilla into a small pan. Then, cut the marshmallows in half and add them to the pan.

5. Gently heat the pan on low heat. Use a wooden spoon to stir the mixture every now and then, until everything has melted.

6. Pour the mixture into the hollow in the middle of the sugar. Quickly stir everything together, until the mixture is smooth.

Smooth the top with the back of a spoon.

Press them in firmly.

7. Pour the fudge into the pan and push it into the corners. Smooth the top, then sprinkle the sugar sprinkles over the fudge.

8. Use your fingers to press the sugar sprinkles into the fudge. When the fudge is cool, chill it in a refrigerator for two hours.

9. Loosen the edges of the fudge with a blunt knife. Then, carefully turn it out onto a board and remove the wax paper.

Try not to knock off the sugar sprinkles.

10. Turn the fudge over and cut it into small squares. Put the fudge in an airtight container and chill it again for two hours.

You could put the fudge into a cellophane bag and give it to someone as a present.

Chocolate truffles

To make about 15 truffles, you will need:

1 cup semi-sweet or milk chocolate chips
2 tablespoons butter
¼ cup powdered sugar
¼ cup vanilla wafers
½ cup chocolate sprinkles
small paper candy cups

Keep the truffles in an airtight container, in a refrigerator and eat them within five days.

You could put the truffles in boxes lined with tissue paper, to give as presents.

Wear oven mitts.

1. Fill a large pan a quarter full of water and heat it until the water bubbles. Then, remove the pan from the heat.

2. Put the chocolate chips and butter into a heatproof bowl. Wearing oven mitts, carefully put the bowl into the pan.

3. Stir the chocolate and butter with a metal spoon until they have melted. Then, carefully lift the bowl out of the pan.

4. Sift the powdered sugar through a sieve into the chocolate. Crumble the vanilla wafers into the bowl. Then, stir everything well.

5. Leave the chocolate mixture to cool in the bowl. While the mixture cools, spread the chocolate sprinkles onto a plate.

6. When the chocolate mixture is firm and thick, scoop up a little with a teaspoon and put it into the chocolate sprinkles.

7. Using your fingers, gently roll the spoonful into a ball around the plate, until it is covered with sprinkles. Put it into a paper cup.

8. Make lots more truffles in the same way. Put all the truffles onto a plate, then put them in a refrigerator to chill for 30 minutes.

Snowmen and presents

To make lots of snowmen
and presents, you will need:

9oz 'white' marzipan,
  cut from a block*
green, red and yellow
  food coloring
toothpicks

* Marzipan contains
ground nuts, so don't
give it to anyone who is
allergic to nuts.

❄ The marzipan needs to
be stored in an airtight
container and eaten
within three weeks.

Coloring marzipan

Add a little powdered
sugar if the marzipan
gets too sticky.

1. Unwrap the marzipan
and put it onto a plate.
Then, cut it into four pieces
and put each piece into a
small bowl.

2. Add a drop of green food
coloring to one of the
bowls. Mix it in with your
fingers until the marzipan
is evenly colored.

3. Add red coloring to one
bowl and yellow to another,
then mix in the colors.
Leave the last piece of
marzipan 'white'.

A snowman

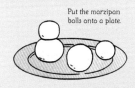

Put the marzipan
balls onto a plate.

Press the ball with
your thumb.

Cross the ends
of the scarf.

1. Roll a piece of 'white'
marzipan into a ball. Then,
make a smaller ball. Press
the smaller ball on top the
larger one, for a head.

2. Roll a small ball of red
marzipan. Press it to make
a flat circle, then put it on
the snowman's head. Add a
tiny red ball on top.

3. Roll a thin sausage from
red marzipan. Wrap it
around the snowman for a
scarf. Use a toothpick to
make the snowman's face.

You could arrange your snowmen and presents on top of an iced Christmas cake.

A present

Make presents from the other colors, too.

1. Roll a small ball from red marzipan and put it on a clean work surface. Gently press the flat side of a knife down on the ball.

2. Turn the ball on its side and press it with the knife again. Keep on turning and pressing the marzipan until the ball becomes a cube.

3. Roll long, thin sausages from green marzipan. Press two onto the cube, in a cross. Then, add two loops in the middle for a bow.

Christmas crunchies

To make about 15 crunchies, you will need:

5 maraschino or candied cherries
8 vanilla wafers
4 jumbo marshmallows
⅔ cup white chocolate chips
2 tablespoons unsalted butter
15 dried cranberries
small paper candy cups

❄ Keep the crunchies in an airtight container,
in a refrigerator, and eat them within a week.

1. Cut the cherries into tiny pieces and put them into a large bowl. Then, break the wafers into lots of little pieces and add them, too.

2. Cut the marshmallows into small pieces, using a pair of kitchen scissors. Add them to the bowl and mix everything together.

3. Fill a large pan a quarter full of water and heat it until the water bubbles. Then, remove the pan from the heat.

Wear oven mitts.

4. Put the chocolate chips and the butter into a heatproof bowl. Wearing oven mitts, carefully put the bowl into the pan.

5. After two minutes, stir the mixture with a metal spoon. When everything has melted, carefully lift the bowl out of the pan.

6. Spoon the chocolate and butter mixture into the large bowl. Then, mix everything well with a wooden spoon.

7. Use a teaspoon to scoop up some of the mixture. Shape the mixture into a ball with your fingers and put it into a paper cup.

8. Make more balls in the same way, until you have used all the mixture. Then, press a dried cranberry onto the top of each one.

9. Put all the crunchies onto a large plate. Then, put the plate in a refrigerator and leave to chill for two hours.

Cool coconut ice

To make 36 squares, you will need:

4 tablespoons of dried or pasteurized liquid
egg white (mix as directed on the packet)
1lb box of powdered sugar
2 cups shredded coconut (sweetened)
3 teaspoons water
2 drops green food coloring
a shallow 7in square cake pan

❄ Keep the coconut ice in an airtight container
and eat it within 10 days.

1. Lay the cake pan on a
piece of wax paper and
draw around it using a
pencil. Then, cut out the
square, just inside the line.

2. Use a paper towel to
wipe some cooking oil onto
the sides and bottom of
the pan. Press in the paper
and wipe the top with oil.

3. Put the egg whites into
a large bowl. Stir them
quickly with a fork for
about a minute, until they
are frothy.

To make pink and
white coconut ice, use
red food coloring
instead of green.

4. Sift two tablespoons of powdered sugar into the bowl and stir it in. Sift in the rest of the sugar a little at a time, stirring it in each time.

5. Add the coconut and water and mix everything well. Spoon half of the mixture into the pan. Use your fingers to press it in.

6. Add the green food coloring to the rest of the mixture. Stir the mixture with a metal spoon until it is evenly colored.

Smooth the top with the back of a spoon.

7. Spoon the green mixture on top of the white layer. Smooth the top a little, then leave the pan in a cool place overnight.

8. Use a blunt knife to loosen the edges of the coconut ice. Then, turn it out onto a cutting board and remove the paper.

9. Carefully cut the coconut ice into 36 squares using a sharp knife. Then, leave the pieces on the board for two hours, to harden.

Marzipan canes

To make four canes, you will need:

3oz 'white' marzipan*,
cut from a block
red food coloring

❄ Keep the canes in
an airtight container
and eat them within
three weeks.

* Marzipan contains
ground nuts, so don't
give the canes to anyone
who is allergic to nuts.

To make a pink
cane, like the one
below, try adding
only one drop of
coloring in step 2.

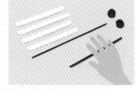

The sticks should be twice
as long as your middle finger.

1. Cut the marzipan into
three pieces the same
size. Then, cut two of the
pieces in half and roll them
into sticks.

2. Put the remaining piece
of marzipan into a small
bowl. Add three drops of
red food coloring and mix
it in with your fingers.

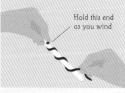

3. Cut the red marzipan
into four pieces. Roll each
piece into a thin stick,
about three times as long
as your middle finger.

4. Starting at one end,
wind a red stick around a
white one, like this. Do this
with all the sticks, to make
three more striped sticks.

Hold this end
as you wind

5. Roll the sticks on a
clean work surface to make
them smooth. Then, bend
the end of each one into a
curve, to make a cane.

Managing editor: Fiona Watt • Photographic manipulation: John Russell
First published in 2006 by Usborne Publishing Ltd, Usborne House, 83-85 Saffron Hill, London, England. www.usborne.com